WOULD RICH MARY JANE
GET ILYANA'S DREAM DOLL?

In class after lunch, Miss Taffy asked the children what they had liked best at Bugle's Toy Shop.

Ilyana smiled and thought of Noelle, the exquisite ballerina doll in a fairylike net of silver and pink.

"I liked the fire engines," said Tommy Kuzlowski.

Mary Jane raised her hand.

"I liked the ballet doll," she said.

"What did you like most about the ballet doll, Mary Jane?" asked Miss Taffy.

"She costs one hundred and seventy-five dollars," said Mary Jane. A few children tittered. But Mary Jane turned and looked straight at Ilyana.

"Of course," Mary Jane added, "that's no problem for me."

YEARLING BOOKS are designed especially to entertain and enlighten young people. Patricia Reilly Giff, consultant to this series, received her bachelor's degree from Marymount College and a master's degree in history from St. John's University. She holds a Professional Diploma in Reading and a Doctorate of Humane Letters from Hofstra University. She was a teacher and reading consultant for many years, and is the author of numerous books for young readers.

Noelle of the Nutcracker

BY PAMELA JANE
ILLUSTRATED BY JAN BRETT

A YEARLING BOOK

To Lucy, whose childhood gave light to this tale.
—P.J.

To my niece Amy.
—J.B.

Published by
Bantam Doubleday Dell Books for Young Readers
a division of
Bantam Doubleday Dell Publishing Group, Inc.
1540 Broadway
New York, New York 10036

ISBN: 0-440-41418-0

Reprinted by arrangement with Houghton Mifflin Company

Printed in the United States of America

November 1997

10 9 8 7 6 5 4 3 2

CWO

Contents

Destined to Dance

I t was December first, and Bugle's Toy Store was bursting with new toys and games. There were bicycles and sleds, model ships with billowing sails, and computers with puzzles to solve. There were leopards and polar bears and teddy bears, and a little pink pig. But the first thing you saw when you entered the store was Mr. Bugle's famous doll collection—"The finest in New York!" Mr. Bugle liked to boast, and it was true! There were baby dolls in frilly lace caps, gypsy dolls with bright calico skirts, and a pirate doll with a red bandana and a patch over one eye. There were dolls with pigtails, ponytails, and long curls like bed springs. The newest arrival was a ballerina doll. Her name was Noelle.

Noelle was a very unusual doll. Her knees and ankles were neatly jointed so that she could bend her legs and point her toes, like a real ballerina. She could do all five ballet positions and stand on *pointe*. Noelle was proud of that. She wore satin slippers with ribbons around her ankles and a silver and pink ballerina's dress that fluttered and floated around her like a butterfly. Her long hair was braided and twisted into a shining coil, and her skin had a faint flush, like a Christmas rose. She was a doll that any little girl would love to own, but Noelle didn't want to belong to a little girl. She had made up her mind from the moment she first bent her pretty leg that she was destined to dance!

"I have a great career ahead of me!" she said to the other dolls. "I am an artist."

"Grunt," said the pink pig. "What is an artist?"

"A great dancer!" said Noelle, and she turned a pirouette.

"Mama! Mama!" cried a baby doll. "I don't want to be an artist. I want a little girl to hold me!"

"That's because you can't twirl on your toes like I can!" sang Noelle.

The pink pig snorted loudly. "Who cares about twirling on your toes? I want to be cuddled!"

"I'd rather be scratched under my chin," purred a blue kitten, waving her fluffy tail beneath her pinafore.

"Not me! Not me!" said Noelle. "I want to dance before hundreds of people in a great ballet. That's what *I* was meant for. But first I must be discovered."

"What is 'discovered'?" asked the pirate doll.

"Like discovering a buried treasure," said Noelle, "only *I* am the treasure."

"I want to be discovered by a little girl," said the baby doll. "Mama! Mama!"

It was seven o'clock and beginning to grow light. The polar bear waited on all fours for children to come and climb on him, and the little pig longed to be squeezed and made to feel piggy-wiggy (which means round and pink). The blue kitten swished her long tail impatiently. Noelle stood quietly on her shelf, practicing first position. But deep down she was hoping and wondering.

Noelle was hoping she would be discovered, and wondering when it would happen.

A Bugle Call

 lyana Ingram listened drowsily to the rattle of trucks on Twenty-fifth Street. She had been having such a nice dream—something about dancing. Yes, she was dancing in a ballet, bobbing and floating like a butterfly, before hundreds of people. Oh, what a delicious feeling it was! She closed her eyes and felt the fairy wings of her dress unfold and lift her up . . . up . . .

Suddenly the living room clock began to chime. ONE! TWO! THREE! FOUR! FIVE! SIX! SEVEN! Even the chimes had a special richness this morning, as if announcing that something exciting was about to happen.

Ilyana sat up and sniffed expectantly, but no warm, buttery smell of pecan rolls or waffles wafted from the kitchen. Then it couldn't be a holiday. Besides, her red corduroy pants were folded neatly across the back of her chair, where Mrs. Ingram had put them the night before, for school.

"You'll probably be up early," she had said, smiling.

Up early! That was it! Today was December first, and Miss Taffy, Ilyana's teacher, was taking the class on a holiday outing to Bugle's Toy Store to see all the new Christmas toys!

Ilyana bounded out of bed and hurried into her pants and sweater, singing to herself.

"Bum bum be-de bum, bum bum be-de bum!"

Patricia poked her head into the room.

"Will you stop making that noise?"

"That," said Ilyana, "is a bugle call! It's a signal to hurry because today Miss Taffy is taking us to Bugle's Toy Store!"

"Oh, is that all?" Patricia yawned. "Wait until you're in fifth grade and you can see *The Nutcracker* ballet. Of course not everyone gets to go. Our class is just lucky."

It was older sisters who were lucky, Ilyana thought ruefully. Ilyana had always longed to see a real ballet. Secretly she liked to imagine that she herself was a prima ballerina—the celebrated Natasha Petrovna! Natasha's double pirouette was a

flash of something winged and white; her famous flying leap—but it was Natasha's famous flying leap that had sent Heinrich, Mrs. Ingram's pet brass bullfrog, flying right out the window! He had fallen five flights and had landed in a puddle in front of the Wing Fat Sing Chinese Restaurant, denting his nose.

"I just got dizzy and lost my balance," Ilyana had mumbled, hanging her head.

"Well, you'll have to get dizzy somewhere else," Mrs. Ingram had retorted. "This apartment is too small for three people and a dizzy ballerina."

Mr. and Mrs. Ingram, Patricia, and Ilyana lived in a "railroad" apartment on West Twenty-fifth Street, in New York City. In a railroad apartment all the rooms are straight in a row, one after another, with no connecting hallways or passages. Ilyana's room was between the living room and Patricia's room. There were six rooms all together, not counting the bathroom, but none of them was very large, and all the furniture stuck out at awkward angles, which made flying leaps difficult, especially for the exuberant Natasha Petrovna.

"It's a good thing I'm so skinny," thought Ilyana,

hastily pulling a comb through her hair, "but I wish my hair weren't so fly-away!" It wasn't at all ballerina-like to have fly-away hair. "If only it were thick and honey-colored like Miss Taffy's, or wavy and red like Mary Jane Igoe's." Mary Jane could twist her hair into a lovely red knot at the nape of her neck, ". . . like a real ballerina." Ilyana frowned and yanked at a stubborn tangle. Whenever she tried to twist *her* hair into a knot, it just popped right out again!

Ilyana continued her bugle song while she pulled on her boots.

"Mom, make her stop that noise," said Patricia, burying a lump of brown sugar in her oatmeal.

But Ilyana was already out the door and halfway down the first flight of stairs. "Bum bum be-de bum, bum bum be-de bum!" she sang as she crunched through the snow to school.

"Children, quiet, please!" said Miss Taffy to thirty-two rambunctious second graders. She was standing on tiptoe, counting them. "Two . . . four . . . six . . ."

Miss Roe, her assistant, was frantically trying to rescue Ellie Berke's hat from several boisterous boys, who were using it as a football.

"Stay with your partners!" she panted in a shrill voice, and Miss Taffy began counting all over again. "Two . . . four . . . six . . ."

Ilyana's partner was Mary Jane Igoe. Mary Jane and Ilyana were always partners on field trips because their last names both began with *I*. Ilyana wished her last name was Brown, or Peterson, or Anastopolos—anything but Ingram—just so she wouldn't have to be partners with Mary Jane. Patricia claimed the easiest way to get a new name was to get married. Ilyana had seriously considered it, but none of the prospects looked too promising. She had always liked William FitzWilliam III, the class naturalist, but William had recently moved to Last Chance, Idaho, taking his *Periplaneta orientalis* collection with him. Tommy Kuzlowski lived right across the street, which was convenient for starting a romance, but the only thing Tommy felt romantic about was fire engines. There was always Elvin Whitechapel, of course—"Adorable Elvin," the girls called him. But Elvin swore that he was going to live in a lighthouse when he grew up, surrounded by girl-eating sharks. Under the circumstances, Ilyana reflected, becoming Elvin's wife would probably not lead to great happiness.

But by the time the class got to Bugle's, Ilyana had forgotten all about wanting a new name.

The boys made a beeline for the machine guns and tanks.

Pop! Pop! Pop!

"Bang, you're dead!"

"Children, please stay with your partners," urged Miss Taffy. But her eyes were just as wide as theirs, and two pink spots glowed on her cheeks.

"Whooo! Whoooooo!" whistled an electric train going around and around, through tunnels and towns. High above, a stuffed monkey chattered from his perch.

"Kekekekekeke!"

Ilyana stopped to gaze at a Ukrainian doll in an embroidered pinafore.

"I have a Spanish doll with four petticoats under her skirt," said Mary Jane.

Next they looked at an Indian doll in a silk sari.

"My Indian doll has real pierced ears," said Mary Jane.

They looked at a Chinese doll and a bride doll

with a wide-brimmed bonnet trimmed with ribbon and lace.

"I'm sick of dolls," Mary Jane said. "Let's look at something else."

They were turning to go when Ilyana saw her. She was the most exquisite doll Ilyana had ever seen, a large ballerina in a fairylike net of silver and pink.

"Ohhh!" breathed Ilyana. "She looks like a flower!"

"She's a ballet doll," Mary Jane said. She was suddenly close to Ilyana, and her breath was hot against her ear. "I don't have a ballet doll. And look, she has real toe slippers." Mary Jane reached out to touch them.

"Don't touch the dolls, girls!" A saleslady appeared from behind the counter.

"I was just pricing her," said Mary Jane importantly.

"I'm afraid she's quite expensive," the saleslady said. "She costs one hundred and seventy-five dollars. She's a most unusual doll. She can do all five ballet positions and stand on her toes."

"Just the way I can!" said Mary Jane, although she was only a beginner at the Beatrice Batten

School of Ballet. She had told Ilyana all about her twelve different leotards and the recital she was going to be in.

The saleslady opened a heart-shaped tag tied to the doll's wrist on which was neatly printed:

"Noelle—that's not a real name," said Mary Jane. "That's a Christmas carol."

"I think it's a beautiful name," said Ilyana softly.

"Oh, I could name her anything I want," said Mary Jane. She was watching Ilyana.

Ilyana was quiet while Mary Jane exclaimed over sleds, bicycles, and an elegant tea set with a border of primroses, all pink and gold. Ilyana discovered a Victorian dollhouse with a grand piano and a shiny brass door knocker. Mary Jane thumped it against the little red door. *Rap! Rap! Rap!*

"This," announced Mary Jane, "is definitely going on my Christmas list."

Ilyana was sure then that she had forgotten all about Noelle.

*　*　*

In class after lunch, Miss Taffy asked the children what they had liked best at Bugle's.

"I liked the fire engines," said Tommy Kuzlowski.

"What did you like best about them?" asked Miss Taffy.

"They go *WHIRRRRRRRR!*" screeched Tommy, making a noise like a siren.

Mary Jane raised her hand.

"I liked the ballet doll," she said.

"What did you like most about the ballet doll, Mary Jane?" asked Miss Taffy.

"She costs one hundred and seventy-five dollars," said Mary Jane. A few children tittered. But Mary Jane turned and looked straight at Ilyana.

"Of course," she added, "that's no problem for me."

Discovery

he day after Ilyana's visit to Bugle's, a young man from the Imperial Ballet Company came into the toy store.

"I've come to pick out a doll for *The Nutcracker*," he told Mr. Bugle with a smile. When he smiled his blue eyes got even bluer.

When Noelle heard *"The Nutcracker"* she trembled from the top of her head to her pink slippers and concentrated so hard on first position that she thought she would break.

The young man, whose name was Bruce Jennings, picked up a baby doll in a ruffled lace bonnet.

"Now *there* is a lifelike baby doll," said Mr. Bugle to Bruce.

"Yes, but a baby doll belongs with a real little girl," said Bruce, and he picked up a gypsy doll with a wide, calico skirt.

"This is a pretty doll," said Bruce, turning the gypsy doll around slowly, "but she is not quite large enough to be seen on stage."

"Oh, on stage!" thought Noelle. "Look at me, I'm just right for the stage!"

Bruce put the gypsy doll back and picked up the pirate doll. The pirate doll glared at him with his glass eye.

"He's a fierce looking pirate," said Mr. Bugle.

"Yes, but he's not quite what I had in mind," Bruce said thoughtfully. And he put the pirate doll back on the shelf.

Then he looked straight at Noelle, standing quietly in first position.

"What control!" said Bruce admiringly. "Even our own ballerinas cannot stand so still."

"Real ballerinas cannot stand as still as I can!" thought Noelle, and a great happiness swelled in her, as Bruce lifted her gently down.

"She's unique," said Mr. Bugle. "She has real joints in her knees and ankles."

"Real joints!" sang Noelle. "I can point my toes. None of the other dolls can do that!"

"Yes, I think she will be perfect," said Bruce. "She

is large and beautiful and will be seen well from the stage with the bright lights shining on her."

"Oohhh, bright lights!" thought Noelle. "I've been discovered at last!"

And Noelle was put in a box tied with string and carried away.

Noelle didn't realize that Bruce Jennings was a prop man for the ballet. A prop man takes care of the things that the dancers will need to use in the ballet, such as toys in a ballet about Christmas, like *The Nutcracker*. In *The Nutcracker* there is always a tall Christmas tree with toys and gifts heaped around it. Bruce had come to Bugle's to buy a doll for the little girl Clara, a character in the ballet, to find under the Christmas tree. Noelle did not know she had been chosen to sit under a Christmas tree. So when she was put in a box and carried off she thought, "I will be the star of *The Nutcracker!*"

While Bruce was congratulating himself on finding the perfect doll for the ballet company, someone else was thinking of Noelle, too. Mary Jane Igoe had not forgotten the ballet doll, and she would have been very surprised to find Noelle missing from the shelf at Bugle's Toy Store where she had first seen her, standing in first position. Mary Jane hadn't the slightest idea what she would do with another doll, but there was one thing she *was* sure of: Ilyana Ingram would never have her.

That very evening, when Mr. Igoe returned from a trip to Hawaii, he brought Mary Jane a Hawaiian doll with golden skin and a wreath of silk flowers around her neck. Mary Jane hurriedly pushed the new doll into her closet with the Indian doll and the Chinese twins and begged her father to take her to Bugle's to buy the ballet doll.

"Absolutely not," said Mr. Igoe, firmly. "You'll have to wait and see what Santa brings."

"I WON'T, I WON'T!" cried Mary Jane turning pale. (Mary Jane was an expert at turning pale.) "You'll go away again like last year, and it'll be too late! I'll hold my breath!"

An ominous silence followed.

Mr. Igoe turned at the sound of a match striking behind him. His wife was lighting a cigarette. She inhaled deeply, watching him.

"What are you looking at me that way for, Nikki?" asked Mr. Igoe.

"Do you want your daughter to hate you for the rest of her life?" said Mrs. Igoe quietly. Mary Jane gave a loud sniff.

Mr. Igoe laughed nervously.

"Not much chance of that, is there, kitten?" he said to Mary Jane. "You know how Daddy likes to tease his little kitty. But deep down he doesn't mean it, even for a minute! How would you like to stroll down to Bugle's on Saturday, after your ballet lesson?"

Mary Jane nodded, and bit her lip to hide a smile.

"That doll is as good as mine," she thought.

A *Secret* Secret

veryone in the Ingram family was busy making Christmas lists. Patricia's was neatly arranged in alphabetical order beginning with "apple blossom eau de cologne" and ending with "xylophone." Ilyana's list was much shorter. It looked like this:

Noelle
Noelle
Noelle
Noelle

"Where's the music?" teased Mr. Ingram. So Ilyana made it look like this:

Noelle
Noelle
Noelle
Noelle

"You'd better put something else on your list," said Mrs. Ingram. "Patricia needs new glasses and I'm desperate for a new vacuum cleaner."

* * *

At school, Miss Taffy's class was planning a Christmas pageant. The theme was "The Spirit of Christmas." The children could choose what they wanted to be, and Miss Taffy would help them make up lines to recite.

"Let's try to be original," said Miss Taffy. "We now have three angels. I think three angels are enough. Can you think of something else you would like to be?"

Tommy Kuzlowski raised his hand.

"Yes, Tommy?"

"I want to be a fire engine!"

The class laughed.

"That's a nice idea," said Miss Taffy, "but I would like you to be something alive, like a wise man. We only have two wise men so far. Yes, Ilyana?"

"I want to be a ballet doll, Miss Taffy."

"All right. Now how does a ballet doll represent the spirit of Christmas?"

"A ballet doll might be given to a little girl who wants to dance and would love her," said Ilyana.

"That's a fine idea. Then Ilyana will be a ballet doll."

Mary Jane Igoe raised her hand.

"Yes, Mary Jane?"

"Miss Taffy, I don't think it's fair that Ilyana can be a ballet doll if Tommy can't be a fire engine. Fire engines aren't alive and neither are dolls."

Miss Taffy looked puzzled for a moment.

"I think you have a point, Mary Jane. Would you like to be a ballerina, Ilyana, like in *The Nutcracker*?"

"I know about *The Nutcracker*," said Ilyana. "My sister is going to see it with her class. It's about a little girl and a wooden nutcracker that turns into a prince and takes her on a magical journey."

Mary Jane raised her hand again.

"I want to be a ballerina, Miss Taffy. I'm taking lessons, and I'm going to have a recital in May."

"We have three wise men; I think we can have two ballerinas," said Miss Taffy. "But remember, your lines must convey the spirit of Christmas."

Mary Jane smiled at Ilyana.

Ilyana frowned and looked away. But she was not really angry. She had an idea, and it was going to be a secret—an absolutely *secret* secret.

After school the next day, Ilyana and Mrs. Ingram went to Fashion Avenue to buy fabric for Ilyana's costume. Snow filled the air, and a sharp wind whipped Ilyana's woolen scarf across her face as they hurried along past the bright windows of the trimming stores, looming out of the dusk like glittering ships laden with treasures—colored glass buttons and beads, ropes of silver and gold, and fine French laces the color of whipping cream. In the fabric stores Ilyana gazed wonderingly at the shelves reaching up to the ceilings, piled high with velvets, satins, silks, and chiffons. But she made her choice quickly—pale pink satin for the bodice of her costume and pink chiffon shot through with silver for the skirt. The salesman had to climb all the way up to the top of the rickety old ladder to reach *that*, but—yes—it was just what she wanted!

That evening she watched her mother gather and stitch the chiffon into a full skirt with a stiff net slip beneath to make it stand out. When the bodice was finished Mrs. Ingram pinned it to the skirt, and Ilyana tried on her new dress. Wisps of chiffon fluttered and sparkled as she twirled across the room, but the pins pricked, so she had to stop.

On Saturday morning, the day Patricia's class was going to see *The Nutcracker,* a Christmas package filled with homemade cookies and fudge arrived

from Aunt Penny. Now it seemed as if the Christmas celebrations had really begun.

"I get all the jelly tots!" said Patricia, tearing off the wrappers and putting two tots into her mouth and three more in her pocket.

"No fair!" cried Ilyana.

"And I get first dibs on the gingerbread men."

"Patricia, share with your sister," said Mrs. Ingram, frowning as she struggled to turn the narrow straps on Ilyana's costume.

"Yum, fudge!" said Ilyana, biting into the dark, rich candy. "Ummm."

"Mom, she's hogging it all," said Patricia. She took six pieces of fudge for herself and went to her room, her pockets bulging with jelly tots. She thought she would have just one piece now and hide the rest from Ilyana. But oh, how good the creamy fudge tasted! She ate two pieces, then three, then four . . . Then she settled down to read but kept thinking of crackle bars and buttercake squares, so she took three of each of those when no one was looking.

Patricia wasn't very hungry at lunch. She felt all right—just a little strange. But when it was time to get dressed for the ballet, she looked positively green.

"Are you all right?" asked Mrs. Ingram.

"Of course I'm all right. Why wouldn't I be? Stop staring, Ilyana! I just feel a little funny." And Patricia burst into tears.

"Owww! My stomach!"

"You must have the flu," said Mrs. Ingram. "You'd better go to bed."

"I don't have the flu," whimpered Patricia, "and I don't want to go to bed. I want to go to the ballet!"

Suddenly Patricia turned chalk white and ran to the bathroom.

"You can't possibly go to the ballet," said Mrs. Ingram, when Patricia was in bed with a thermometer in her mouth. "I'll call Mrs. Schumeyer and tell her you won't be coming. And don't say a word until I take that thermometer out of your mouth!"

"You don't seem to have a fever," Mrs. Ingram said to Patricia after she had spoken with her teacher. "But you look awful." She put her hand on Patricia's forehead.

"It isn't the flu," gulped Patricia. "It's all the c-cookies and fudge I ate." And she hiccupped.

"Mrs. Schumeyer suggested that Ilyana might like to go, since there is an extra ticket," said Mrs. Ingram.

Ilyana looked from her sister to her mother, her eyes shining.

"L-let her have my ticket," said Patricia, hiccupping.

Ilyana felt like jumping up and down, but she didn't because her sister looked so funny and awful lying in bed with her eyes all red and puffy, and hiccupping. And she wasn't really such a bad sister. At least not all the time.

Magic Glasses

n the Great Hall with Mrs. Schumeyer's fifth-grade class, Ilyana leaned forward, gripping the railing of the balcony. Below her were hundreds of people—she could look down and see the tops of the ladies' hats, black and red and green and gray, small knitted caps and elegant felt hats worn at sophisticated angles. Above her the chandeliers slowly dimmed, as the overture ended with a tinkling of bells, and the curtain rose slowly on Act One of *The Nutcracker.*

A murmur rose from the audience, "Ahhh!" The scene was a large, old-fashioned living room, and in the very center, blazing with candles, stood a magnificent Christmas tree. Icicles of twisted glass glittered in the boughs hung with fruits and toys. On the very top was a gold angel. The candlelight danced in her gold skirts as though she were twirl-

ing in the tree. Beneath the tree, toys and gifts were piled high.

A young girl skipped into the room. Her long hair was swept back by an immense bow, and she wore lace bloomers beneath her dress, like a picture Ilyana had once seen of her great-grandmother as a little girl. The girl, whose name was Clara, picked up a large doll sitting beneath the tree and began to dance, her lace skirts fanning out like a white flower.

"I want to dance like that!" thought Ilyana, sitting on the edge of her chair. As Clara turned a *fouetté en pointe*, something glittered in the lights. It was the doll's dress.

Ilyana felt a tap on her shoulder, and Mrs. Schumeyer leaned over and whispered something that sounded like "magic glasses!" Then she fumbled in her purse and brought out a pair of opera glasses, which she handed to Ilyana.

Ilyana held the glasses up to her eyes, but everything was so far away now! Even the candles on the Christmas tree were just tiny dots of light.

Mrs. Schumeyer nudged her gently.

"Turn the glasses around," she whispered.

Ilyana turned the glasses around. Then, magically, she was right in the middle of the festive, old-fashioned room. Cabinets of dark, polished wood gleamed in the firelight. (The fire was a make-believe one of colored paper, but it glowed just like a real fire.) Candy apples glistened on the tree, and a gingerbread man bobbing from a branch winked a raisin eye. In the corner of the room stood an enormous grandfather clock. Through the glasses Ilyana could see that it said quarter to eight, exactly. A delicious shiver ran up her spine. She, Ilyana Ingram, was *really there*, in a fairy-tale house of long ago, where strange and wonderful things could happen.

Clara's red shoes flew across the stage. Suddenly Ilyana was looking into a delicate, familiar face, framed by a coil of shining hair.

"There's Noelle!"

Mrs. Schumeyer put her finger to her lips and shook her head.

Ilyana was careful not to speak out loud again as she gazed through the wondrous glasses at Clara's dancing partner. She knew the rich, glossy hair and rosy skin; even the pink slippers were the same. It just had to be Noelle!

The clock struck eight and guests began to arrive for the Christmas Eve festivities. The children ran

to open their presents, while the ladies, with their bright fans fluttering gaily, danced a minuet with the gentlemen. Suddenly, a mysterious figure in a long, black cloak and tall, peaked hat swept into the room. It was Clara's godfather Drosselmeyer, an inventor, bringing all kinds of fantastic surprises from his enchanted workshop! The children crowded around as he threw back his cloak and revealed his first triumph: a doll as large as Clara that came to life and danced.

"I'm sure Noelle would be a wonderful dancer, if she came to life," thought Ilyana.

Drosselmeyer's gift to his goddaughter was a wooden nutcracker. Enchanted, Clara pranced coquettishly around her new toy.

In the second act, Clara and the nutcracker, now transformed into a prince, danced through a glittering forest of silver firs to an enchanted city of candies and confections, where streets paved with sugared almonds wound around turrets and towers of brown sugar spice. In the gardens ballerinas floated through the "Waltz of the Flowers," their pastel skirts lifting and falling like petals in the breeze.

Gradually the Tiger Lilies and Morning Glories

folded their petals; the light changed from gold to a soft, luminous blue, and Clara and her prince were adrift on a starlit night. Clara's long hair streamed in the wind, and the dew glistened like stars in her dress, all blue and silver. The prince lifted her in his arms, and her thin dress fluttered like an evening flower opening its petals to the night. Just as the sky began to blaze with rose and gold, old Godfather Drosselmeyer came to take Clara home. The sunbeams turned her dress into a ripple of gold as the curtain fell.

Suddenly everyone was applauding and shouting, "Bravo! Bravo!" Mrs. Schumeyer's fifth graders stood and shouted, too. But Ilyana sat perfectly still. She couldn't believe that the ballet, with its beauty and magic, could simply vanish behind the curtain. And what had happened to Clara after old Drosselmeyer carried her away?

The applause was deafening and the shouts of "Bravo!" louder than ever. Ilyana watched, fascinated, as the curtain rose and the Tiger Lilies and Morning Glories returned for a bow, wide-awake and smiling in the bright lights. Drosselmeyer and the prince came back and stood together like old friends. Last of all Clara returned, and a bouquet of roses was laid at her feet. Then the lights came on and people began talking and laughing and shuffling into the aisles, just as though they had never visited the fairy realm of *The Nutcracker*.

Ilyana brought the whole ballet to life for Patricia at home that evening, especially the moment when she recognized Noelle through Mrs. Schumeyer's magic glasses.

"It wasn't the same doll, silly," said Patricia, sitting up in bed with a bowl of hot chicken broth. She wasn't eating any more of Aunt Penny's fudge.

"It was Noelle; I'm sure of it," said Ilyana, spinning and stumbling into Patricia's desk.

Patricia was thoughtful as she blew on the steaming broth. "Next," she said, "you'll be telling me the doll danced, too."

On Monday during recess a small group of girls gathered around, enraptured, as Ilyana related the story of how she had discovered Noelle dancing in *The Nutcracker*.

"Maybe it wasn't really the same doll," said Ellie.

"Why don't you go to Bugle's and see if Noelle is still there?" suggested Lizann.

"She's not there," said a new voice. Mary Jane Igoe stepped forward. Ilyana had not noticed her standing behind the little knot of girls. "She's not there," she continued, "because my father took me to Bugle's to buy her, and she was gone. I figured Ilyana was getting her for Christmas!" Mary Jane smiled slowly. "I'm sure glad my father is on the Board of Directors of the Ballet. Thank you for telling me where to find her, Ilyana."

Ghosts and Shadows

lyana stood motionless as Mary Jane turned and walked away. The girls gathered closely around her.

"What board is she talking about?" asked Ellie.

"She's probably making it up, whatever it is," said Lizann.

"I bet she's not," said Ilyana. "Her father is friends with the mayor. He probably has this board, too."

"Well, I don't see what an old board has to do with the ballet and her getting that doll," said Phyllis.

"Maybe she means a Ouija board," said Lizann. "My sister has one of those."

"Oh, why did I have to go and show off about the ballet?" wailed Ilyana.

At that very moment, something exciting was happening at the ballet company. Old Mrs. von Borden had donated Cassandre, an antique doll, to the ballet. Cassandre was a French doll, one hundred and ten years old. She had a china head with yellow china curls, a wide straw hat, and a lace dress.

All the ballerinas who were rehearsing gathered around to admire her.

"An antique!"

"Oohhh, look at her hair!"

". . . at her hat!"

". . . at her dress!"

"A gift from Mrs. von Borden!"

"Can we put her in *The Nutcracker*?" asked one.

"Oh, can we?" entreated two others in chorus.

"Clara can dance with her!"

"Ah, *oui*," said Nanette, the French ballerina. "Clara and Cassandre will make a charming *pas de deux*" (which means, in French, "a dance for two").

So that evening Clara pirouetted and twirled with Cassandre, as she once had with Noelle.

But what about Noelle?

Bruce Jennings, the prop man who had bought Noelle for the ballet, had orders to put her in storage.

"Oh, what is storage?" wondered Noelle. She had enjoyed dancing with Clara, and she had loved most

of all the applause, which she was sure was meant for her.

"Storage?" said Bruce to himself as he carried Noelle to a dark room behind the stage. Noelle's eyes looked large and frightened.

"It doesn't seem right when you could make some little girl so happy," he said aloud. "But to shut you away in a dark box until next year—or maybe—forever . . ."

"Dark box? Forever?" thought Noelle. A cold, heavy feeling crept into her limbs.

But Bruce didn't shut Noelle in a dark box—at least not then. He left her on a shelf and went away and shut the door.

When Noelle's eyes became accustomed to the dark, she saw she was not alone in the room. She could dimly see shapes of other toys and dolls around her. But they did not speak. They only sighed, and their sighs seemed to say:

"Forever!"

"So long we can't remember . . ."

"In the dust . . ."

"In the shadows . . ."

"Without little hands to hold us . . ."

"STOP IT!" Noelle screamed. "Stop it! Who *are* you?"

But in the prop room there was perfect silence. Nothing stirred except a spider spinning a web across a cloth doll; it had made a nest in her hair.

Time passed. To Noelle, standing in the strange silence of the prop room, it seemed like a long time. Days and nights slipped by without much to distinguish them except a patch of gray light that shone through a small, high window in the daytime. Noelle could see that next to her, around her, on all sides of her, were dolls and toys, even a stuffed donkey with long, floppy ears. But these toys did not talk and laugh like those Noelle had known in the toy store. These toys, gray and covered with dust, had given up hope. Sometimes Noelle heard such strange sighings and shufflings that she thought she would go crazy. Once she tried to talk to the gray donkey.

"Please, Donkey, who are you, and where are you from?"

The gray donkey said nothing. He just hung his great, shaggy head. But deep in the night Noelle heard mournful, hoarse voices, chanting:

> *Beware, beware*
> *Of the grime and dust.*

Or you'll become
Ghosts, like us!

"Who's there? Who's there?" cried Noelle. But no one answered her.

Noelle stopped trying to talk to them. Fear hung heavily in her heart. Would she become faded and gray, too? Perhaps her lovely joints would rust, and she would not be able to bend her legs and point her toes anymore. She began to think about what Bruce Jennings had said when he'd brought her back to this strange room.

"You could make some little girl so happy!"

Noelle had not thought of making Clara in the ballet happy; only of how delicious it was to whirl in her arms before hundreds of people until she was blissfully dizzy. Now Noelle began to think of a little girl holding her in a different way, perhaps dancing with her, too, but because—*because she loved her.* It seemed to Noelle, while she stood in the gloom, a faraway dream of happiness.

"Once we knew children!" sighed the toys.

"I knew the sweetness of little arms!" murmured the cloth doll faintly through a cobweb.

"But how will I ever escape?" wondered Noelle.

The cobwebs brushed across her, and she did not like it at all when a long millipede crawled slowly across her silver dress.

A Beautiful Secret

t was December twentieth, and the Christmas pageant was only two days away. Ilyana's costume was finished, and she had been working hard on her lines. Every night at home she sat at her desk, chewing her pencil and crossing out words, until her wastebasket overflowed with crumpled paper. Finally she was finished.

"My lines are going to be a surprise," she told Miss Taffy.

"That's fine," said Miss Taffy. She was busy helping the three angels with their lines.

"What's your ballet costume like?" Mary Jane asked her.

"It's a secret," said Ilyana.

"My mother is buying me a new costume from Dancin' Dandy," said Mary Jane, "and ballet slippers to match."

"Mine is a secret," said Ilyana.

It was a beautiful secret, too. Ilyana stood in front of
the long mirror in her parents' room the night of the
pageant. Mrs. Ingram had brushed her hair until it
shone, and she had dabbed rouge on Ilyana's already glowing cheeks. The new dress stood out over
the crinkly slip like pink and silver tissue.

"You sparkle like Jack Frost!" said Mr. Ingram.

Ilyana made a face. "Daddy, I don't look like a
boy."

"You look like the doll you described in the ballet,"
said Patricia.

Ilyana wiggled her toes in her new ballet slippers
and said nothing.

At school there was great excitement and con-
fusion backstage. An angel had lost her wings and
was crying pitifully, and the wise men were throw-
ing spitballs at each other.

"*Baa! Baa!* I'm a lamb!" bleated a little figure
bundled up in a fur coat. "*Baa! Baa!*"

Ilyana took off her coat and boots, adjusted her
ballet slippers, and ran to the lavatory to fluff up her
skirt. She hardly recognized the ballerina in the
mirror, with her bright eyes and silvered skirts.

Why, it was the great Natasha Petrovna making her American debut! How sublimely she twirled—faster and faster! Behind Ilyana the lavatory door opened, almost silently. It was not until she had stopped twirling and was deep in a bow that Ilyana realized someone was watching her.

"Don't you look pretty, though," said Mary Jane sweetly.

"Thank you," said Ilyana, straightening up quickly. Mary Jane was wearing a gold dress and matching slippers; her flaming hair was coiled on top of her head and crowned by a little gold tiara. But she looked strange. It was the way she was staring at Ilyana.

"You know what you remind me of?"

"What?" said Ilyana.

"That ballet doll! You look exactly like her! Of course, you wouldn't be a doll, because we aren't supposed to be dolls, are we? Which reminds me, my father is back from Japan and he's promised to speak to the Board about—"

"Oh, shut up!" said Ilyana, flushing hotly. Before she knew what she was doing, she pushed Mary Jane as hard as she could. Surprised, Mary Jane

staggered backwards against the door. The color drained from her face and her eyes narrowed.

"I'm going to make you sorry for this," she muttered. She grabbed Ilyana's skirt and pulled . . . and pulled. Suddenly there was a sharp tearing sound, and part of the skirt came loose at the waist.

Just then the lavatory door opened, and Miss Taffy burst into the room.

"Oh, there you are! Ilyana, you're right after the angels, don't forget!" Then she stopped. Her eyes fell to the torn skirt.

"What's going on here?"

No one spoke. The two girls glared at each other. Mary Jane's face was ghostly white, and Ilyana felt as if her cheeks were on fire.

"What kind of Christmas spirit is this?" said Miss Taffy. "Mary Jane, go help Ellie find her wings, and hurry! Thank goodness I have safety pins."

Miss Taffy went to work quickly while Ilyana blinked back hot tears of anger.

"I hate Mary Jane," she thought, her heart pounding. "I *hate* her! She's ruined my dress and spoiled everything!"

"What happened?" asked Miss Taffy, her mouth full of pins.

Ilyana swallowed hard. Her throat ached and

tears burned her eyes, but she didn't want to cry in front of Miss Taffy, no matter what. "Mary Jane is always bragging that her father can get her anything, especially things other people want," she said in a choked voice. "I got so mad I pushed her, and then she tore my dress—*on purpose.*" Ilyana's voice cracked. Miss Taffy just frowned and went on pinning, the wrinkle in her forehead growing deeper.

"Miss Taffy doesn't like me anymore," Ilyana thought miserably. A tear trickled down her face, but she whisked it away with her tongue.

"There," said Miss Taffy finally, standing back. "At least the rip doesn't show. The angels are going on now, so hurry and remember, 'Way up high.'"

"Way up high, way up high," Ilyana said to herself over and over. "I must remember, 'Way up high.'" Backstage she could hear the angels chanting:

> *We are angels*
> *In the starry sky.*
> *We sing our praises . . .*

They stopped. There was dead silence in the auditorium. Someone giggled backstage, and then one angel pushed another and giggled, too.

"We sing our praises . . ." one angel began uncertainly.

"Way up high!" all three finished in chorus (or almost in chorus).

Applause followed and the angels fled. Ilyana walked on stage. She was sure she'd be able to see her family in the audience, but she couldn't recognize a single face in the harsh glare of the lights. All she could think of as she stood there was how triumphant Mary Jane would be if she forgot her lines. Suddenly she realized she really *had* forgotten her lines. And no one knew them, not even Miss Taffy. She had been too careful to keep them a secret. Ilyana stood blinking helplessly into the blinding lights.

There wasn't a sound from the audience. Then suddenly a small voice piped up. "Is she a doll, Mommy?"

There was giggling backstage and a commanding, "Shhh!"

"But I *am* a doll!" thought Ilyana joyfully. And making a stiff curtsy, she began loudly and clearly:

> *I sit under a Christmas tree*
> *Just as quiet as can be.*
> *Though I cannot change my pose,*
> *I dream of dancing on my toes.*

But when I'm held by a little girl
I twirl, and twirl, and twirl . . .

And Ilyana twirled right offstage to a thunder of applause.

Miss Taffy was waiting for her in the wings with a big hug and a "Congratulations!" Beside her stood a handsome young man.

"Miss Taffy," said Mary Jane, hurrying up to her teacher, "Ilyana cheated. She wasn't supposed to be a doll. You said so, didn't you?"

But Miss Taffy, with her young man beside her, only smiled, her face flushed.

"Yes I did, but Ilyana surprised us," she said. "She was a doll who comes to life when a little girl dances with her. I think it was a nice surprise, don't you? Perhaps it would be better if you thought more about your own lines, and stopped worrying about Ilyana."

Mary Jane bit her lip and looked dangerously pale.

The young man with Miss Taffy was looking intently at Ilyana.

"You reminded me of something I'd almost forgotten," he said, smiling. When he smiled his blue eyes got even bluer.

Noël!

t was Christmas Eve. On the steps of St. Patrick's Cathedral, carolers gathered, their voices lifted exultantly in the sharp air. Up and down Fifth Avenue people stopped to look in the lighted windows of Saks, where miniature figures in long coats and fur caps strolled down snowy, lamp-lit streets, stopping to gaze in the windows of *their* department stores. In the Great Hall, Clara and Cassandre, the French doll, danced their last *pas de deux* of the season. And at the Ingrams', Ilyana and Patricia were making popcorn balls.

"This one is for Daddy," said Patricia, putting aside a robust popcorn ball.

The sound of carolers drifted up from the street below.

"Noël! Noël! Noël! No-o-ël! Born is the King of Israel!"

"I wonder if Mary Jane Igoe will find Noelle under

her Christmas tree," said Ilyana dreamily, as the voices faded away.

"When you're my age, you'll forget all about dolls," Patricia said, licking her fingers.

"Girls, it's almost ten o'clock," Mrs. Ingram announced. "Time for bed."

"Oh, can't we stay up and wait for Daddy?" pleaded Ilyana. Mr. Ingram had disappeared into the cold night shortly after dinner.

"Go to sleep and when you wake up it'll be Christmas, and we'll all be together," replied Mrs. Ingram.

So Ilyana and Patricia went to bed. Ilyana fell asleep and dreamed she was dancing in Gingerspice Square. She broke off a morsel of scalloping from a house made entirely of Tipsy Cake (it was still warm from the oven) and was just about to pop it into her mouth when a dancer wearing a black mask and a glittering gold dress snatched it away and began to dance around her, chanting:

> *Ha! Ha! Ha!*
> *You should see*
> *What I've got*
> *Beneath my tree!*
> *All things here*
> *Belong to me!*

The masked dancer dissolved in laughter, which faded into a shrill whistle. Ilyana awoke to the familiar whistling of steam in the radiator. The first faint light was stealing into the room. Very quietly she got up and tiptoed into the living room where the Christmas tree stood, its tiny blue lights winking like stars in the boughs. Two bulging stockings hung from the bookcase (which became the chimney on Christmas Eve). One had an *I* embroidered on it in red, and the other a *P* in green. Ilyana stood up on tiptoe and peeked in the one marked *I*. Suddenly the floor creaked behind her, and Patricia appeared in her nightgown, rubbing her eyes.

"I thought I heard you!" she whispered. "C'mon, let's take down our stockings!"

Ilyana found a chocolate Santa, a bar of strawberry soap, a new comb and brush, and a locket with a tiny pose painted on it. At the very bottom of her stocking was a small, flat envelope. Inside was a piece of paper, and on it was written:

WHOEVER DISCOVERS THIS LETTER
IS ENTITLED TO ONE YEAR OF LESSONS
AT THE BEATRICE BATTEN SCHOOL OF BALLET

Ilyana began to dance around the room, waving the paper.

"I discovered it! I discovered it!"

"Merry Christmas!" Mr. Ingram stood in the doorway in his bathrobe. Mrs. Ingram smiled sleepily behind him.

"No dancing in the living room!" she said. "Miss Batten said you can practice all you want at the school."

"I'm going to practice every single day," said Ilyana.

Patricia found a book for her under the tree, *The Story of* The Nutcracker. Mr. Ingram promised to take her himself next year, just the two of them. On the first page was a picture of a Christmas tree hung with fruits and toys and gingerbread men, just like the one in the ballet.

Soon a sweet, buttery fragrance mixed with something spicy floated from the kitchen. Mrs. Ingram was making waffles and frying sausages. Behind the tree something glinted mysteriously. Curious, Ilyana crawled around the tree . . . and around . . . to where Noelle stood on the very tips of her pink toe slippers.

For a moment Ilyana just stared. Then she reached out, and very, very gently, as if she expected Noelle to disappear in a puff of pink smoke, she picked her up. There was something reassuring about the shining softness of her dress and her satin slippers. They were *real*.

"I can't believe it!" she said over and over.

Mrs. Ingram came from the kitchen with a wooden spoon in her hand and a dab of flour on her nose.

"Miss Taffy's fiancé certainly liked your performance in the Christmas pageant," she said.

Ilyana looked in bewilderment at her mother and then at her father and Patricia.

"He's the prop man at the ballet!" Patricia burst out. She had been keeping the secret since the night before.

"When Bruce saw you at the pageant, he remembered the doll he'd put in storage," explained Mr. Ingram, "so he resolved to ask the ballet's permission to give her to you. He wasn't sure the ballet would agree, especially in time for Christmas. Then last night, when we had almost given up hope, he called and told me to come get her!"

"But it's just like magic," said Ilyana.

"Just like magic!" thought Noelle, tingling with happiness.

Mr. Ingram looked at Ilyana in surprise.

"Bruce told me the very same thing," he said.

Christmas night, when everyone was in bed, and New York lay glittering in the cold starlight, Ilyana tiptoed into the living room, carrying Noelle. The Christmas tree looked mysterious, its pale stars glimmering through the dusky boughs. Ilyana held Noelle close, pressing her cheek against the doll's shining hair. Noelle smelled good—new and sweet.

"Here is where I found you," Ilyana whispered, "and if I hadn't dressed up like you in the Christmas pageant, and played a doll coming to life, I wouldn't be holding you right now. Just think of that!"

But Noelle was thinking her own thoughts. Her silver dress shimmered in the starlight and her arms bent lightly, lovingly around Ilyana. They seemed to be urging her to . . . to what?

"To dance," whispered Noelle.

And *that* was the beginning of a real *pas de deux*.